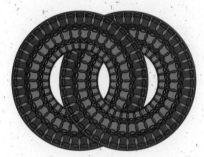

THROUGH
A GATE OF TREES

THROUGH
A GATE OF TREES

Susan Jackson

poems

CavanKerry ◊ Press LTD.

CavanKerry Press Ltd.

Fort Lee, New Jersey

www.cavankerrypress.org

Library of Congress Cataloging-in-Publication Data

Jackson, Susan, 1947–

Through a gate of trees : poems / Susan Jackson.—1st ed.

p. cm.

ISBN-13: 978-1-933880-02-0

ISBN-10: 1-933880-02-3

I. Title.

PS3610.A3522T49 2007

811'.6–dc22

2006037266

Cover art by Donald Kilpatrick III © 2006

Author photograph by Stephen Taylor Photography

Cover and book design by Peter Cusack

First Edition 2007

Printed in the United States of America

NEW◈VOICES

CavanKerry Press is dedicated to springboarding the careers of previously unpublished poets by bringing to print two to three New Voices annually. Manuscripts are selected from open submission; CavanKerry Press does not conduct competitions or charge reading fees.

CavanKerry Press is grateful for the support it receives from the New Jersey State Council on the Arts.

Acknowledgments

Thank you to the editors of the publications in which these poems first appeared.

"Black Ice" in the *Paterson Literary Review*

"This Light," "In Johore Bahru," and "Night Walk" in *SOUTH MOUNTAIN*, An Anthology of the South Mountain Poets

"On the Old Road," "Bringing Home Potatoes," and "Praise for Washing Feet" in *NIMROD* International Journal

"The Man Who Could Not Talk About the War" in *Eleventh Hour Stories*

"What the Silence Feeds" in *NIMROD* International Journal

With thanks

To Joan Cusack Handler for her grace and vision and to all at CavanKerry Press.

To Molly Peacock for her sure guidance, encouragement, and generosity of spirit.

With appreciation for the sensibilities and insights of Marjory Bassett, Diana Beach, Joanie Brady, Sondra Gash, Mike Stanley, South Mountain Poets, and all who gathered for the Spring Lake Retreat.

Thanks to dear friends who bring me deeper into poetry every day.

To Poets & Writers for their fine support and my compatriots at the National Arts Club.

With gratitude to Deena Metzger for Daré. Thank you to Stephen Dunn for the ever present reminder to "Walk Light."

With thanks to the New Jersey State Council on the Arts, the Geraldine R. Dodge Foundation, and the Virginia Center for the Creative Arts.

Notes

The title "The Twittering Machine" is taken from the Paul Klee painting.

Poems on pages 19 and 69 refer to notes made while listening to the Dalai Lama's "Training the Mind/Opening the Heart" at the Beacon Theater, New York City, August 12–15, 1999.

The epigraph for "Indigo Sky, New Moon" is from Thoreau's journal, March 21, 1853.

for my family
and those who came before us

and for you

Contents

Foreword

In the poems of Susan Jackson, animals appear at key moments, escorting us to a truer world. Jackson quietly depicts the realms of social obligations—family, marriage, children, parents—as places of constriction and sacrifice. These are realms of nights where cars skid on ice, where adults lie awake, where children startle. But inside these worlds she secretly prepares places where an animal, a fish, a turtle, a snake, a fox can enter. And when they do, the fact of their being supplies each poem with a greater truth than any social twisting of the self into an acceptable form. Animals always accept their forms. What is more at home in its shell than a turtle? What more comfortable in its skin than a snake, who knows just when to shed it?

In the work of American women poets like Emily Dickinson, Marianne Moore, and Elizabeth Bishop, animals step up at the exact moment when a truer or more natural self is called upon. The animal, not the social self or the self that is shown to others, but a robust entity full of its own being, testifies both to the depths of an experience and to a boundary where that experience meets the ordinary world. In Emily Dickinson's poem "I heard a Fly buzz—when I died—" a fly "interposes" between death and life to vivify the transition between these states: "There interposed a Fly—/With Blue—uncertain stumbling Buzz." In "The Mind Is An Enchanted Thing" Marianne Moore presents the shimmer of thinking as "the glaze on a/katydid-wing," or a "kiwi's rain-shawl." References to these creatures prepare the way for Moore to activate the word "true" into a verb in the middle of poem, where the world is "trued by regnant certainty." In Elizabeth Bishop's poem "The Moose" a bus, that most social of ways to travel, stops for the antlered being to inspire the awe of existence in the bus riders, bringing them all to a threshold of being more consciously alive. These poets' sensibilities seem to form some literary family ties for Susan Jackson's receptivity to the world.

Jackson partakes of her literary great-aunts' legacies in this, her first book of poems—although she has been writing, but not publishing in book form, poems all her life. To me, *Through a Gate of Trees* is about the mental discipline it takes for a social being to insist on the difference between social bonds and being bound. The work aims for those states of being fully alive, of being spiritually aware, of existing as the animal of the self might exist, undistracted by the human guilt of love's demands. The poems take place all over the world, yet wherever they are, the situations are domestic, and the stanzas flood with memory, with obligations, and with the dilemma of how to recognize what exists underneath the pleasant surfaces of things.

Beyond the lawn chairs and badminton net of a garden "In Johore Bahru," a dog keeps barking, and its owners are exasperated until they realize the annoying dog has found a true threat, "the cobra rising/from the red hibiscus." "A Boy Visits His Uncle in Contadora" takes place on the deck of a boat where a great fish "flaps about wildly/as if it could find water again," horrifying the boy, whose "small mouth gulps for air/like the fish." The preoccupied uncle seems immune to the suffocation of the fish until the boy's shouting—like that dog barking at the hibiscus—finally urges him to act to prevent more pain and "he at last takes out/his clean, sharp knife." Jackson, like her subjects the dog and the boy, alerts us to sharp truths beneath the mindless actions that cover up suffering.

Life beneath the surface is always Jackson's interest. Like her literary aunts, she is both a serious witness to the world and a bemused one. In "Visiting on Cape Cod" she positions the reader in the guest bathroom. In her first line she situates us with a slow pan of her discerning eye: "There is a framed black and white picture of her father," she says. But with the second line she bursts out, "above the toilet. Perhaps she is so pissed off at him/that this is the perfect place."

In my favorite poem, the witty "We Are Learning to Dedicate Our Lives to Compassionate and Selfless Action," she attends one of the Dalai Lama's public engagements, listening "to a translator/shrivel words into a different language." Jackson watches the Dalai Lama, who has been suggesting to the audience that they "let go/of worldly attachments/. . . of the baggage we carry," finish his speech and leave, followed by a monk who "totes gently" the guru's "small cloth bag." She finishes the poem by imagining the contents of the bag—even a great spiritual leader has to carry a purse—"nothing heavy,/notes, reading glasses, perhaps/a packet of Kleenex. . . . "

The combination of focused, amused attention to detail as well as the sudden appearance of a saving animal underpins the structure of the poem that gives the collection its title, "How I Got Here Through a Gate of Trees." Here the speaker numbers and lists sixteen stages of her life, in one, two, or three long-lined stanzas, from birth through childhood and adolescence, and into adulthood. In stanza fourteen she realizes "There are countries for which we have no passport" and in stanza fifteen "leaves her husband, finds the way back with pockets of sea glass." It's only by the final stanza that "One morning something lifts like smoke and disappears into the sky." That ineffable "something" I can only take as a placeholder for the ways in which we refuse to listen to our instincts.

Then, a bit like Bishop's moose, a "red fox crosses into the meadow." But where does it go? As in a realized fairy tale of the self, it ventures to a threshold, that edge between the ordinary and extraordinary that the lyric poet seeks. Dickinson puts a fly at that boundary, a "stumbling buzz." But Jackson chooses "a gate of trees," where at last she can divide obligation from imagination. It is through this gate that the fox disappears, and Jackson seems to follow him. Because that gate is made "of trees," it suggests a magical forest where the poet's spirit might be able to shine in complicated subdivisions, like the wings of the katydid in Marianne Moore's poem. With the gate of trees Jackson seems to find the place of "an enchanted thing," and we as readers can follow her over the threshold to that truer world she searches for in this debut book of poems.

—Molly Peacock
Toronto

THROUGH
A GATE OF TREES

EARLY MORNING IN THE GARDEN

It matters how you come to a thing.
Even a blade of grass is sharp
from a certain angle.
The quick spade driven into ground
can slice earthworms in half.
Only some grow back
what they have lost.
Weeding exposes a slug tucked
like the sad underbelly of happiness
to the cool place where lily stem meets soil.
Leave it be this time.
Pull from another place.
Who disturbs the wild thing
may also find the bee,
off on its own errand, dangerous.
It matters how you come to a thing
or let it come to you.

PRAISE FOR WASHING FEET

It was all I could have wanted of resurrection,
at that moment,
the fluid jug lifted to the basin, pouring
water so it landed with a sound like flutes
through the spruce trees, their cool
spacious gestures roused by wind.

You scooped the water in both hands
and splashed my two feet,
rounding, rinsing between toes,
the slow massage moving over
arches, heels, the soles
until we lay back in startled praise
for hands, and that cool water.

But today I come in almost too tired
to lift myself up the stairs,
know nothing at all to bring
what I need back to life,
unless it's our day of the fluent hands,
the earthenware jug splashing
water like flutes; yet here I'm far away
and the only praise I know now
is to go again in some singular way
to a metal faucet and a small white basin
and let the abundant water flow
into my own two hands.

IN JOHORE BAHRU

In its glazed pot
the moon flower,
petals closed up against
the sun and still
so white on the terra cotta tiles
outside the shade porch.
The amah brought our tea tray
to the rattan table
where we sat round in silence
holding the cold glasses
to our palms.
Heat trickled down leaves
and everything which could
lay quiet through this
afternoon as smooth
as a keeper of secrets.

The badminton net was abandoned,
lawn chairs left
till the heat would pass.
Everything sucked inside itself,
then Jake's bark
urgent, furious.
Suddenly you hissed *ssh*
quiet but he kept on barking
and barking until we got up
to go and look
and found the cobra rising
from the red hibiscus.

THE MAN WHO COULD NOT TALK
ABOUT THE WAR

He grabs her arm, seizing her from sleep
at three a.m. *Don't move.*
There's someone here. Next to us.
She looks into the darkness
then again to his face, filled now
with transparency, carried back
to the jungle, to the ambush.
Her eyes search the vacancy
of moonlight on the window.
It's a dream she tells him.
We're all right. Go back to sleep.

He sinks back to silent breathing
until suddenly he flings his arm
across her shoulder. *Stay where you are*, he shouts.
This place is full of mines.
Help them, help them but she cannot
see the bodies or hear the sounds they make.

She lies in the narrowness
of one side of the bed,
touching his hand until light
seeps through the window across the contour
of the no one who is there.
Waking, he reaches for her
and turning to him she thinks
of the things that can be shared:
a table, a bed.

BRINGING HOME POTATOES

Lifting their rounded nubby bodies from the bag
moist and dirt grab the air.
They are not actually damp but still
speak the dark damp language
of underground, of earth
covering, touching them as they expand into it.

Could we have the same unstraining patience
growing eyes, waiting in the dark
unable to breathe in anything other than
this peculiar way of knowing that
everything is as it's supposed to be;
so sure of the inevitable harvest?

BEAUTY IN FORM

Last Monday a litter of feathers
settled in a sort of circle
in the garden beside the house.
Now this afternoon you follow
a sudden sound,
an alarm cry, high-pitched, rapid,
"ee" "ee" "ee"
to the window
where a hawk
has a small bird
in its talons.

You bang on the window
and the hawk
half jumps half flies
to the other yard
where it tears its hooked hawk beak
into the screaming bird.

This is the same dark wing span
you watched framed
against blue sky, soaring,
beauty in form
you thought.

Hawk being what it is
rips apart bits of flesh
small bird unaware in a moment
prey

no heart-beating body,
strewn feathers matted on the grass
in a sort of circle;
you never see bones.

REMEMBER RILKE

Remember Rilke said *every angel is terrifying*
or did you expect joy without risk
radiance decanting like wine
or perhaps you would rather be mulled
with cloves by an open fire
until you resonate with heat—
yet even here you are
still separated from the fire
by the golden bowl.

You wish it could be simple,
the bit of soap left
at the bottom of the bath
wiped away in a single sweep
as if we could turn as easily
toward what we want,
toward the mysteries
lying beside us at night
like husbands and wives.

FIRST SPRING IN A SEPARATE HOUSE

1.

The garden all full of lurch and promise
as she pulls away some dead leaves
and fills the beds with mulch.
Shoots hint at daffodil and crocus.
Faithful earthworms turn to task,
churning the invisible darkness for
what comes next. The plum branches
have grown tiny red buds she notices
before going back inside
where the too-perfect rooms wait quietly.

2.

He comes one evening to talk
and they are nervous as school kids.
He arrives at her door with jonquils
cut from the garden she left,
a bouquet yellow and bright,
wrapped in a damp paper towel;
she has fixed the meal he likes.
Asking polite questions they nod
and reminisce over what is safe,
alternately eager, then cautious,
each so careful of the other,
leashed together by the density
of this fragile space between them.

3.

Mornings alone—a spill of stones, one shell
beside the deep tub, the china parrot he gave her
stalwart on its stubby branch, bright eyes watching,
watching. In the shower she lets hot water wash
over her body for a long time
as what is remembered washes over her too,
rituals of morning in other places . . .

4.

At the Great Barrier Reef they once ate mangoes
each day for breakfast, melon color wedges
in round white bowls, nights full of moon
and sea turtles nesting the beach,
birds rustling in the trees.

Sometimes later at home he would cut the flesh
away from the pit, slice a mango crisscross
and arch the skin so each half opened like
a flower he would bring to her on a plate,
like an offering.

Tonight she visits, brings him mango
whole, smooth, skin green and crimson.
In return, he gives her grapefruit
round and heavy, to take home;
this exchanging of fruit
saying something
they can't quite speak yet
in words.

EASTER WEEKEND

Chance guests in the same house
she spent the evening next to a man
side by side on the arc of couch for
a rented film. The silver play lasts,
they search for comfort on the old wicker sofa,
cushions unforgiving, the distance between them
becomes so little they forget to take care
the odd elbow or knee should not touch.
Pillows shift to cradle heads and feet extend
over the good footstool, these two
in the TV light as if alone in a bed as intimate
as any long or tender marriage, so many hours spent
in front of the screen, shared laughter in all the right places,
a glance of disbelief, the raised eyebrow when their chosen
hero or heroine does something really over the top.
He loves movies. She only a novitiate to the higher
order. Later he might instruct her on the nuance
this director looked for in his exemplary cast.
Or be tempted to retreat to the chosen
more familiar solitude of his borrowed room.

ICE STORM

There was a night like this when I was too small
when the sound of the wind in the trees
kneaded me into thinking it could come inside
and snatch me from my bed.
My sister and I could hear short raps
on the window
as sleet staccatoed against
the casings meant to protect us
and all night my two hands
held their fierce grip on the quilt.

Now, years later,
I discover the wind comes dressed in the disguise
of your body
with your hands and your smile
so that I will be beguiled into going of my own accord
never realizing until too late
moving like a somnambulist to the soothing tone
of your words,
indeed the same song the wind sings
and I should be afraid.
How hard to give fear a name
how easy to confuse the sound and the wind
and think the howling comes
from outside.

Tonight as the temperature falls ice hardens,
the silence in the snow is deep and round
and all the trees are made of glass.

THIS LIGHT

This whiteness absorbs
all the first light
from the opening sky
and carries it back across the air,
creating a trick, an illusion:
dogwood petals in early morning light
like April snow
resting on the tree branches,
reminding me
of other small deceptions,
fear as hatred,
longing
as possessiveness.
But with practice
could we learn to live
on the land, simply
like snowfall
or dogwood blossom,
so this light flows through us,
finds us,
lets us know its joy.

WE ARE LEARNING TO DEDICATE OUR LIVES TO COMPASSIONATE AND SELFLESS ACTION

The Dalai Lama tells us to let go
of worldly attachments, our grasping
and desire, let go of all the baggage we carry.
But here in life's airport signs everywhere
say leave no baggage unattended.
I picture my little travel bag of fear,
the duffel filled with what ifs. And see,
it's all been monogrammed and tagged
to follow me through each change of planes
and new gate. If I simply leave it,
walk away, it will be confiscated,
sniffed at by trained dogs
who know what to look for; pried open
by officials who will see
just how it's been packed, with what
haste and uncertainty some of it
was stuffed in at the last minute
just in case it might be needed.
One can't foresee everything.
I'm willing to give up quite a bit
but what about the books I bought
especially for the trip? The white dress?

And after renunciation what?
All day I listen to a translator
shrivel words into a different language—
enlightenment is not confined

to one lifetime alone,
but is this a comfort?
I know it's not about being idle
or extravagant, which often I am,
or even exuberant joy
unable to contain itself beneath a saffron robe.
He doesn't speak of grace
but in the lull of the moment
I wonder how should my heart
open unless it's here and now?

His Holiness looks up, today's teaching
ends as he descends the dais,
smiling and bowing to those he passes.
Move simply without encumbrance
a body could say.
Then there's the Dalai Lama's
small cloth bag: nothing heavy,
notes, reading glasses, perhaps
a packet of Kleenex, which another
monk now retrieves, totes gently,
without pride; no, the bowed head,
serene expression. With reverence, I think.

JUST LIKE ME, THESE OTHER UNKNOWERS

Under the mimosa tree in the side yard
I would squat or sit on the giving ground.
Long before reading or writing
I drew pictures with half a stick,
different lines to echo sounds I knew.
The earth was brown and flat
and I could tell it my enormous stories.
I didn't even need to coax them—
symbols moved into little groups
and became words. I thought I had pierced
the world's secret language
with my broken stick and hoarded
the discovery for myself.

Now in Egypt, on the windy road
from Thebes to Abydos, scholars say
they've found the earliest alphabetic
writing carved in limestone cliffs
where ordinary people wanted
what the scribes had, that sweet
knowledge written on papyrus,
so they made something new using
sound symbols—my wavy lines
for M! My stick person, arms raised
to the sky—Ha—becomes H!
Just like me, these other unknowers,
their insistent scratches over soft stone
or earth—what a savage human thing
this writing down is, how it makes us live
each day as if the world will last.

THREE GREEN APPLES AND A PEAR

Three green apples and a pear
in a blue bowl on the table
in the kitchen. Two pears,
spoiled inside, already
in the garbage.
The fly in the ointment
Mother used to say,
but I never saw the fly,
mistook ointment for anointment
and the only time I'd heard that word
was in church, *he anointeth me with oil*
which didn't sound good either
but somehow it sounded like being chosen
and I wanted to be chosen,
especially if it meant beloved,
if it meant beloved
that's what I wanted.

I wanted to be told
but that wasn't anointing
that was annunciation—
the voice of God or an angel
with a lily in her hand,
but the faces in the stained glass windows,
the people being told in paintings . . .
they looked terrified
and after all
the voice of God!
How could you be sure
of what you heard?

THE TRIAL

Don't know why she is alone,
a child in the little den with its unlit fire,
the too-big cherry desk anchored
like a weight at one end of the small room,
with a picture window to the woods beyond
where in the early days of discovery
Mother taught her to name the plants—
jack-in-the-pulpit, lily-of-the-valley,
crown vetch, but outside it is dark;
the curtains already drawn
when she sits alone on the floor by
the blue leather arm chair.

The eerie light spreads
from the squat, square box with its
four splayed legs and glassy face
where she sees a man named Adolf Eichmann
on trial. The child wonders for what? *Crimes
against humanity*, the television says.
She's caught in quicksand, drawn
into the shadowy glow
of the small screen, into the pile of naked bodies.

She is afraid they are human.
She sees arms, a round bald head. She has no voice
but what escapes in little throaty gasps
too small for what she sees,
she puts her hand to the glass
to see if she can touch them.

BLACK ICE

Tantalized by the silver rings of smoke
encircling us, watching them disappear
into the wainscoting above our heads,
I must have been eight,
tired of sitting still so long on the Windsor chair
in her living room, listening to my grandmother,
the aunts, my mother. Their voices
always clipped, abbreviated to hide meaning,
coded into the secretive rustle of the unsaid.

I slipped away like the smoke,
up the stairs to the window seat on the landing
where I could listen without being seen.
Tracing the pattern on the blue velvet cushion
round and round with my finger tips,
I caught snatches of *sad*, *blame* and other words
I had no way of naming.

Don't go there they'd said but in the billowing
afternoon something pulled me to the brass
doorknob, to the dusky cool of the attic stairwell,
a mull of fear and anticipation brimming
in me like a voice from another language.

Grime cut what light might have come
through the small round windows.
By the chimney an old mahogany table
with a burn mark,
a flowery tea set thick with dust.

Behind a stack of *National Geographics*
on the floor I saw a rectangular cardboard box
with the image of a china doll on top.
Inside there was nothing

but old letters and a newspaper.
I saw Grandma's face before I understood
the headline with her name, beneath
the picture of a boy my age, words
"killed instantly" swimming across the page,
"April ice" "car skidded." *This, this* I thought.
This is what it is and I didn't hear the footsteps,
there was nothing but the sudden hand on my shoulder
as I turned into my mother's face,
the narrowing, angry eyes.

INSIDE OUT

he thinks he remembers times when she wasn't sick
but just before his mother died
he got used to being quiet for long afternoons
playing Legos while she slept
stuck in the waiting even though it hurt
as little bits of energy burst out of him like flares
and once he kicked over
the chair

when he closes his eyes now
there are flashes that flicker and pass so fast
he's not even sure he saw a light
just that woozy feeling and his body goes taut
with a want for her to be
the way she used to be
hairs prickle down his back and arms
when sometimes he thinks he can smell her then
the pining turns from a slow spread over everything
to explosion and he would try anything
to get away from it

keep moving he mutters
as he knocks the ball into the trees
he's eleven now
he wants it to snow
and goes out early listening to ice crackle under tires
as cars begin their slow descent down the road

NOCTILUCA

for Peter

You come back with the children
for the first time since she died.
New creases around your eyes,
you remember everything,
remember Contadora,
how she knelt on deck
cleaning the amberjack we caught
trawling, scales shimmering in the sun
as she flung them onto the wood;
the day we anchored off Saboga,
swimming in the shoals you found
a field of red starfish, almost too late
we saw the sharks, their triangle fins
black, circling in on us.

A BOY VISITS HIS UNCLE IN CONTADORA

It's hot in the boat and the man
squints at the line
as he reels it in, straining
all the while against what tugs
from the other side,
finally raises the amberjack;
pleased the fish is this big,
he releases it on deck.
The fish flaps about wildly
as if it could find water again,
as if the slapping sound
of its own body thrown against wood
urged on the empty gills,
the staring eyes;
but it's the boy's eyes
that have the desperation
and the high pitch in the voice.
But he's not dead. This is mean.
You're hurting him.
Kill him or throw him back.
Don't let him suffer!
His small mouth gulps for air
like the fish
like the fish flapping
the boy's bare feet pat
back and forth on the wet deck.

Do something! the boy shouts again.
Kill him or throw him back in the water.

Just don't let him suffer this way.
The man wants to say *it's our dinner,*
calm down or even *shut up!* but as he starts
to speak something moves in him,
the pain that's part of life, then
as if he were seeing
into the boy's own future,
some inevitable suffering to come
that might still be prevented,
he at last takes out
his clean, sharp knife.

DISSECTION

I started with tadpoles as a child, using a straight pin for a scalpel,
or maybe a needle from Mamie's sewing box, summer days beside

our fish pond on the little stone patio under the trees. It was just as hot
inside the classroom that afternoon when we sat at lab tables,

slightly woozy from formaldehyde, some none too eager to perform the deed.
Sally Chasnoff held onto her rat's paw as if the silly thing might up and run away.

I sliced straight down center, then pinned each side of the frail rubbery skin
to the flat board underneath. Two found hearts still beating, by reflex

the teacher reassured them. Betsy Bradshaw's had an opaque sac filled with
pokey protuberances, these would-be babies were moving she screamed.

I inserted a pipette through my rat's half-cranked open mouth and nudged
it carefully down the windpipe then (ugh) put my own mouth to it,

puffed the soft inflation of each spongy lung still bubbly and moist. We
pushed aside the tiny carnelian liver and uncoiled bowel, gently lifting

with our skewer-like metal tools, the pulse of the room more and more quiet,
a sudden air of secret probing, something almost furtive between each person

and their body; the pale pink, my rat's private parts—the time we'd
hid in the attic, one girl standing guard by the top step watching the door

while the rest of us in turn took a silver mirror to our vaginas,
trying to get a good look at this hidden lively place between our legs.

Someone who knew because she had an older sister told us
the hole could open big enough for babies to come through

but Suzanne Barnes, who knew everything, said it wasn't true
and I jumped, almost knocking my beaker over when the teacher interrupted—

time's up for today class, her sing-song voice telling us
this is how we learn, boys and girls, hands on, examining the body.

THE SECRET HISTORY OF ROCK AND ROLL

We wrote it in one wild month in a place Peter found on Ibiza.
In those days the whole island was full of crazy people
making music, making art. We'd lived the story so we decided
to write it all down. We had this idea we'd just get to work
but hell, it wasn't easy transcribing that stuff onto paper.
Nothing wanted to squeeze into any one dimensional
kind of size. But I've got to say the guys had vision.

Somebody built a fire on the beach and somebody else
started playing a little music, people were glowing and
smoking a little. Seemed like the wind quivering,
coming up off the water, rolling right over us, tasting
like salt, and the dancing, everybody moving like some kind
of mystery just jumped into them. The fire, the dancing, drinking
a little wine, arms and legs burnished with perspiration,
everybody looking mighty edible.

The partying and writing would go on just about
all night—somebody would get an idea, somebody else
saying *yeah I remember* and add something else
and we'd be flying.

I think we pretty much got it all in this book.
Sometimes, though, you've got to hold onto secrets
a while. Some people gone on, some trying to live
a different life. I'm not saying I agree totally—you know,
about keeping secrets—but we've got to think about the kids,
let them go to school, not get hassled. I'm not saying we don't
own those lives. We did it. There's nothing we didn't do.
And we made music. Man, we changed the fucking world.
You'll read all about it.

BY SOME STRANGE CONJUNCTION
after a line by Russell Edson

By some strange conjunction my mother had mice for sons.
She needed offspring that would stay smaller than she was,
and besides, she ate people for breakfast so this kind of progeny
had obvious advantages, in addition to lending our family
the air of embracing a full spectrum of the tame and the wild.
Of course she knew it could have been a calamity
had my father questioned the long tails or beady eyes
but as it was she never told him much in the first place.
She might have at least said something like darling,
don't you think it's nice we have mice for sons
but he probably would have said yes dear and IBM
went up three points today. He had a head for figures
and often vanished into them for long periods of time.
Once when the boys scurried through the room, playing
tag on the kitchen counters and hide and seek in the dishwasher
he thought they'd come from the neighbor's to sleep over
and play and just never gone home again.

Whatever she finally told him he thought was all right because
my mother reminded him of his mother, particularly
when she shrieked or threatened to put muzzles on those boys.
Which I thought she would have been justified in doing.
I thought they got away with murder most of the time.
More than once when she sent Jack back to the kitchen for corn
he sat in the fruit bowl instead, eating cherries then tracking juice
all over the floor with those hideous little tap tap paws. He thought
he was so cute. I guess I really shouldn't speak ill of the dead.
I don't think it ever would have happened if my mother hadn't . . .

well, it just makes me sick to think about it, but what can you do, some things just can't be helped and well, we're still a happy family and what mother in the end doesn't squash at least one or two?

THE HUSBAND AND WIFE, A FABLE

They spoke to each other through the voice of their only dog
who often barked or whined her anger and bit the husband

once or twice. Still they were a couple devoted to one another
and to the dog. They lived a life, had friends in, traveled.

Of an evening with the three together by the fire the husband
might tell the dog how hungry I am, tell your mistress

it must be time to fix dinner, or she might confide
in the dog your master is certainly demanding today

but always in the sing-song playful voice of gesture
made in fun, of almost no account that anyone could see.

The wife loved her dog despite increased snarls, the pacing
tempestuous moods and the husband loved

his wife. He fed the dog some herbs designed to soothe.
He tried to please his wife and make the dog well,

but it soon became more restless, frenzied, sleepless
and suddenly one night died. They knew something

but could say nothing. Silence they must have thought
was better. And some months after the dog was gone

abruptly the husband packed a bag and left. A thing with
no voice always sickens and dies, or finds a way out.

VISITING ON CAPE COD

There is a framed black and white picture of her father
above the toilet. Perhaps she is so pissed off at him
that this is the perfect place. She says they
have not spoken in years. In the photo he is smiling,
jaunty, one leg crossed over the other, a hand
waved in the air, some kind of gesture of story telling
or familiarity, a hand possibly about to reach out to touch
and maybe this is what she is afraid of
one slap too many or a father's hand where
it does not belong but I would have no way of knowing
and am a guest here who does not know how to ask such
questions, only to witness. While some fathers watch
over a desk or dresser or even the back of a grand piano
hers is above the toilet amidst the yellow and red flowers
of the peeling vinyl wall paper in between the sink
and the shower. Perhaps he did not shower her with love
the way a father should, the kind of person a girl would
want to call Daddy with the kind of voice that says "my
Daddy said such and such" or "my Daddy took me to the zoo."
Perhaps the home was already a zoo, the kind where you hope
you can slip into the house quietly and make no noise until you are
in your room with the door locked and this is definitely not the kind
of person you would call Daddy, especially not "My Daddy."

BLUE

Blue hospital gown twists
and winds around me
as I turn from side to side,
moving toward the blue hour
of your birth; inside my belly you
swim past women with blue basins
on their hips going to the river to bathe,
past Mary Magdalene clasping her blue shawl
as she rushes into the cool blue Jerusalem morning,
you pass hills blue as the Serengeti at sunset,
your forefathers' blue sails lifting
in the wind as they head out to sea;
as you swim past blue starfish
in the reef shoals my temples pulse,
blue drums beat, I pant as I push you through the
blue currents of your ocean world into
light dazzling your new eyes child of the blue hour
air beating into your lungs till you cry out
the hymn of your arrival into the new homeland
you make for me in your coming.

AFTER THE TWINS ARE BORN

After the twins are born and safe,
bathed and bedded in their nursery cribs

my face turns white as snow
blood pools, you run, doctor

slaps my face, calls my name,
but I am under water, under snow

room goes, I drowse, sleepy
I remember stories of travelers lost in snow

mesmerized by cold they lie down,
though sleeping means freezing

slipping, falling, smiling
nothing matters now

room gone, light gleams
so bright, reminds, recalls me

to the white bed, the radiant room
light like a prayer wheel

light the wheel, hands warm,
here, let me hold my babies

THE DAY SHE GETS HER LICENSE

The car is as long as a city block
and sleek
the fins stretch out as far as the eye
can see
or so she imagines.
It's the early days
of metallic finish
the color of the car
blue frost or silver
depending on the way
light glints
off the surface
or how high
the sun is.
With the top down
the red leather seats shine
like the inside of a flower
like a flag in the wind
and her hair trails out
behind her, flying.
When the guy on the corner,
the cat with the long side-burns,
looks across the street
and whistles
she knows it's for her
she knows
she's beautiful
she will always be
beautiful.

IN MY DAUGHTER'S KITCHEN

As if cleaning could make things right
I take down the small glass bottles
blue, green, rain-water, one by one
from the window ledge
where chimney soot has settled
with the dust rising up from
the street here to the 20th floor
while steam and sun streak the sky
with color in this undulating afternoon.

My daughter's leg will heal
we feel sure of it
even though she's groggy with pain
and fitful right now.

As I rinse the sponge in the sink's
soapy water, soot blackens the porcelain
reminding me how mangoes
planted next to coffee fields
take on a coffee flavor.

I wish I had mangoes to offer her today,
I think, as I watch the shining cars
stream down 2nd Avenue
their flow mesmerizes me in the moment,
this day captured like a photo on her wall,
this photographer daughter

and maybe when she wakes

I will ask please one day
when you feel better
take a picture of all this
the lights, the cars, the darkness,
somehow our life.

Before closing the curtains
I stand by the lamp,
momentarily framed, arms
raised to the invisible sky,
silhouetted in a window of light.

WATCHING THE PERSEID METEOR SHOWERS

We spread our quilt against
the dewed grass, enveloped
in the domesticity of darkness

in the overflow of silence
where night dissolves into blue air
trees shimmer as

the moon opens
bats dart across tree tops
beyond their brushing wings

our eyes scan the trail
of Cassiopeia and Perseus
watching for the sudden

glint of a moonlit needle
drawn into night
meteors come and go

as quickly as bliss sometimes
a flash, a splurge
then the light is lost

your breath
like a small bird
as meteors skid the sky

and disappear like that!
as dazzling
as anything you might

wish for, an approach,
or the sudden wind of change
on an ordinary day.

THE STORY THE REPORTER TOLD

tfor Donald LeGarde Jackson, 1917–1945

He didn't like getting up so early,
leaving them while they slept.
She'd be up soon with the baby,
but still, he decided not to go back
to the room in case he woke her.

All the way to the airfield in his face
the sun rising over the ocean.
A good chill to the morning,
too much maybe, for April.

When he got to the hangar they told him
there was a man, a reporter, came all the way
from New York. Wanted to see the guy
who'd taken down so many planes in the Solomons.
"Could I go up with you?" the man asked.

He said sure, explaining how he felt
every time they lifted off the ground,
the euphoric breaking of bonds, the way
the sky speaks up there, the way the earth
draws away. He pushed the throttle in.

It was the engineer who first smelled
smoke. The crew worked at what they needed
to, doing all they could do;
quick, quiet, intent. For a moment did he
see her face, hear the baby cry?

The other engine coughed, then quit,
within seconds the plane in a
spin, what did he see then, one wing threading
downward, in the moment when he knew
they would hit the water,
and go under.

WHAT WAS, WHAT COULD BE

I have no dark secret things
to tell about my father
except to say he was born
to a family already lost,
his mother crushed
by her first born son dying
so quickly of the fever
she could hardly bear to look
at another blue-eyed boy.

At home he felt ignored, shunted
so he grew a self wide,
kind, exuberant with others
and occasionally volatile.
Things could rise and fall away
in a moment,
anger, love, often sorry,
but I would have suffocated
without him,
though we always lived
in the shadow
between what was
and what could be, curdled sometimes
by how needy perfection is.

Those generous, hunched shoulders,
blue veins swelling the back
of a hand
like tributaries carrying

the living river.
So today I bring flowers
to his grave
and to the brother beside him.

FIRE IN THE BRAIN

What knowledge made my father so afraid
of fire? Always asking did you turn off the stove?
Unplug that toaster?
Once in a restaurant forty-five minutes
from home he looked at me and asked
if I had put out my last cigarette just before we left
but I couldn't be sure.
Images of fire engines, house blazing
plagued me all the way home.
Why I quit smoking I think.

Fire, the last enemy, with the power
to take away the things he loved.
He installed heat sensors and smoke detectors
from basement to eaves
but fire came in a way he never expected—
fire in the brain as if what we protect against
has the power to come anyway.

Tumor—*rushing through the cells like wildfire*
the doctor said—
etched away memory, the meaning of things,
loosened the anchors of time,
the diurnal pass of light and dark
no longer fixed his body to the proper places
of rising and resting.

We watched radiation singe his cheek,
hair fall out; when almost everything

had burned away
he passed the fire on to me
where it burns in a slow smoldering
called grief.

ALL DAY THURSDAY

Quick, quick she keeps saying but it isn't.
Her eyes cease focusing here
and hold a continual fix on something
over there in the corner near the ceiling
invisible to me
but she tries to speak to this presence
and sometimes lifts her arms
as if reaching out to it.

I sit on a needlework footstool next to the bed.
When she can no longer sip water
through the bendable straw
I moisten her lips with a small sponge
the way they do for people with fever
or during a long labor.

Toward afternoon every part of her
devotes to a kind of holding back against the exhale,
then a shallow rush of air out.
This continues with rasps
and occasional high whistling sounds
from deep inside. I am afraid
and I'm glad I am with her.
As day diminishes,
the room begins to shrink.

Now her eyes close,
not so much soothed by my words
of comfort I think

as no longer able
to both look and breathe.
She is held now in the reflex
in out in   out
with the pauses between longer
and longer
and several times I think it might be over
then suddenly it is
I am left cradling the hand, the face,
and the breath
has set her free.

IV

COPPERHEAD

It appeared at the edge of the woods on Gregory Lane,
moving through the grass toward the swing set.
He was planting red buds, packing dirt
with the old iron shovel which he brought down
quick and hard just in time to kill the snake.

Both hands slack at his sides he came
to the back door to tell me what he'd done,
ask me to come and see if I knew what it was.
Copperhead? Don't tell the kids, he breathed.

I knew it was dead but still took a step
back. The only other time I'd seen
a snake so big was in Malaysia when he'd
come on R&R from Vietnam, where
they'd seen some poisonous ones themselves.

Maybe he lifted the pummeled thing
on the shovel's spoon and threw it
in the woods or maybe he buried it.
So long ago. I don't remember now,
but the other night after a nature show on seals
he suddenly said *Remember that snake?*
I wish I hadn't killed it.
I think we still have the shovel hanging
on a rack in the barn next to the rake
and a couple of ancient hoes.

WHAT I HEARD AT FOUR O'CLOCK

It was only an experiment in telepathy.
You said you would think of me at four o'clock
and ask me later what I'd heard.

I hadn't expected to be driving home
listening to radio weathermen call the surprise
storm one of the century's worst.

The day-long build-up of heat
meeting an oncoming rush of cold air
would account for the lightning and wind.

I could hardly distinguish
one word from another in order to link them
into phrases or explanations.

There was thunder and such a pelter
of rain pulling the car to the roadside
was the only thing to do.

Did I hear your voice? Perhaps
after all it is true that people hear
what they want to hear

that what happens in the formative years
shows itself later on in reactions
as solid, say, as a pyramid,

or circular and circuitous as vines.
We may go back trying to sort Tuesday
from Wednesday or Friday, wondering

was it here that it happened,
that feeling as if coming out of Egypt,
willowed with exhilaration,

or we may only think we imagined it
like a dream and wonder in silence
do we deserve a sign of this magnitude?

As if the world could be taken apart
stone by stone and reconstructed in safety
like Abu Simbel, shored above the water's

edge, but instead it's as if we arrived in Paris
to find no Tour Eiffel, Notre Dame gone,
our only cathedral the river and the rain.

But in the hymn of river and rain we listen
for some message, or simply the wind pulling us
toward what we didn't know we wanted.

WHO SEES THEM

In the room where the woman lies in her bed
her first husband hovers near the ceiling
watching as her mother and father
emerge out of the far wall to save her
with their secret hands,
remembering how they used to hold her
when the little girl woke from a dream
and the apple tree where she played
grows all the way up one corner of the room,
branches bending close enough to touch;
beneath these wide wings
she once built forts and pretend houses
before the real houses opened their doors.

But here visitors come, her children
with their children, women bringing flowers,
nurses carrying trays and oxygen tanks
the daily traffic moves and sways like the dreams
of all that has happened or could have happened,
someone pins on a corsage—for the prom,
yes, the lavender chiffon dress, another
places the new baby in her arms, someone
kissing her a long time by a creek where
the air smells like wild strawberries,
and water rushes over stones.

Outside the window a wooden bench
in a snow covered garden;
the roses gone, lavender dried to sedge,

perhaps iris bulbs nestle in the earth
but in the room the sound of voices
in the hall muffled by the heavy door
and even though the television is on
to a tennis match
as she lies in her bed dying
all these other things are happening too
who sees them—
the blue spinnaker hoisted, billowing,
the wind she feels in her face?

BORDER CROSSINGS

A hazy dream, the green couch where children huddle
and I follow you. Then this light everywhere.

It's cold, old-tired I doze in the ungrateful bed
long before morning, confused by this vision of light,
remembering how Mark Doty found a crab shell
sky blue inside and wondered where inside us
is there a window open to heaven and Lucille
says she has also seen the light and heard the voices.
Lucille and I, we are sisters. She is teaching me how to say
what I see, how to say I've seen something
like Komunyakaa's *god awful wind* all lit up, blazing,
not stopping when the dream ends or now when I
blink my eyes, when the bony vessel of myself breaks open.
Someone said only in what's broken can there
be cracks enough to see the light through.
Rain. Soon everything will be muddy and wet.

For now everything's still luminous, light filling
the room and I remember being thrown from a horse
as a child, yelling "Mama" as I flew through the air,
calling out to the one who couldn't answer, "Ma"
like a goat's bleat, "Ma" for the source of comfort,
until "Ma" the world is calling back,
"Ma" it calls, cradling me in arms of pure light.

MOTHER OF MEMORY COME
UP FROM THE WELL

An old woman
has lost her way
to the memory house.
She waits for words
to return like morning,
she puzzles after
what ferments
in an empty bowl.

Tell me Mother
where your house was.
What shall we look for
in the deep woods.
I search your face
for some flicker,
in the still, cool waters
of the well.

Mother let me
stay a while,
let me wait with you
till the ancient pail
spools down.
Mother,
let me
hold you.

Night turns

into itself over
and over,
stars gleam,
then extinguish
in the light shafts
of daybreak.

POEMS SOMETIMES COME IN THE
WAY A SEA TURTLE LAYS HER EGGS

She heaves her way up from the sea,
hauls the heft
of her dark body
to keep an ancient promise;
when she comes to trust
the silence
she starts to dig:
flippers swat and scoop
a bowl,
grit flies back . . .
my bed is a white boat
she tells the moon's eye
as eggs
smooth as river stone
accumulate in sand.

Each turtle lays once,
then heads off
in the unruliness
of exhaustion
leaving the hidden nest
to uncertainty—
predators, weather—
but in time
under the slender auspices
of darkness,
hatchlings spill out,
the beach grass teems

with baby turtles
puzzling their awkward way
toward water,
shiny black bodies crawl
over each other
overflowing in the moonlight
so many, so small,
the first splash,
night and the ten thousand
new living things.

I SLEEP ALONE IN THE METICULOUS NIGHT

Alone in Denmark, Tycho Brahe scanned
the night sky, charted the position of 777 stars,
one brighter than Venus in Cassiopeia he found in 1572—
the sky muse surprising him like me when

the red fox appeared from the woods
I had thought empty of surprises.
How do we learn to receive these offerings,
mango, pomegranate. Don't balk I tell myself.
Learn to name things by their qualities: big sky,
luminous tree. How often I've looked over
the precipice without jumping and don't know why.

Emerson said power resides in these moments
of transition. Uncertainty too. Perhaps disorder
is only what can make you cry. I sleep alone in the
meticulous night. We're capable of everything.
"If I had wings like a dove" says the psalm's tender offering.

I once saw written in dirt on the back
of a pick-up truck "Elvis lives in Houston, Texas"—
tidbits informing the world, they're liminal
space like a porch or veranda—wherever you
are at home in the world will give you safe passage
to the next place so you can re-feel, re-member, repair.
Keep an alms bowl on the desk to invite what comes
to come. Outside dragonflies set off in the flittering
of their exemplary wings, the mystery of grace.
Lavish your entire eye on just this provisional

moment. I remember thinking once we could be safe.
Fastidious patience, something would be right. Not what
eats at people. The air is salty today. And restless.
Clouds grow tails, the hurricane is coming. Fish have
been poisoned by something in the seaweed, maggots feed
on what washes up. A bird with yellow wings. How to
separate what we can't see from what we can, the beautiful
from the ugly. They have changed the locks on the gate.
I'm tired of always looking for the good. Something's
punctured. I shiver in the impossible light.

There's a point of light in the deep northern sky like nothing
ever seen before reverberating its radio of light like rings
on the universe's dark pond. Right here dusk shimmies
in the thicket and the tree frogs are racketing loud
as the train almost. In the sutra teachings allowances
are made for certain instances of attachment and desire.
The Dalai Lama says "although born of desire the practitioner
should be free of the pollution of desire." That's distinction.
There's discernment for you. The world's beauty, here for us,
pure as the round white moon on any summer evening, like
tonight.

INDIGO SKY, NEW MOON

"We are affected like the earth,
and yield to the elemental tenderness."
—Henry David Thoreau

In tenderness

indigo sky

and new moon

speak the same

language

of your eyes

in wordless ways,

that rare

form of Braille

only eyes

can feel:

how extravagant

the smell

of almond blossom,

its wide white

branches,

your eyes,

new moon

slivering

indigo sky.

THE STONES BELONG TO THE LAND
for Henry Munyaradzi

The stones belong to the land.
Henry Munyaradzi says God made them—
he feels the spirit of abiding presence
in rocks, water, trees; all things
possess this light.

Henry chooses stone without the thickness of desire
neither wanting
nor not wanting, listening,
for not only the hand must come to it
but the whole being
from its deep place,
touching the same deep place
in the stone.

In such communion
the chisel begins its task
here and here and here,
the places where the stone calls
the hand frees an eye, a cheek,
the curve of a mouth

until carved and sanded like this
the new form is placed
by the open fire in the yard,
close to the flame where its pores
open to the heat, smolder.
When the stone is so hot

he can barely touch it
he rubs beeswax onto and over
until the wax seeps into the hot stone
which he polishes
until a sheen comes up,
rising to a slow gloss.

HOW I GOT HERE THROUGH A GATE OF TREES

1. They won't let me go at first when I am born. Mother goes home without me.

2. The little girl slips into the early morning garden to watch halos of light around the blades of grass.

3. The secret language of words.

4. I learn that love also means *be good be quiet say please* and *thank you*

5. We move north.
   Sometimes the news is bad and I don't understand.

6. My sister and I find what's hidden in Gramma's attic.
   In school Egypt and Rome.
   Poems grow in a red notebook.

7. My body becomes a new thing and how it's touched.
   He goes to war.

8. I believe in love and wear the white dress.
   We sail on a boat for France, to poppy fields and familiar harbors from the old paintings.

9. I am a mother. Babies come two at a time and are beautiful. We cradle them and laugh in our abundance.

10. *One two buckle my shoe three four shut the door five six pick*

up sticks sing, nurse, plant,
wash, walk, dance, cook meals, find patience.

11. I offer myself to the dark. I am blessed.
    We have a garden and I meet a prince.
    The baby dies.

12. Father is away on business when the smallest one puts broken
    glass in his nose so we stay in hospital
    overnight. I don't write that day either.

13. Belgium. Portugal, a revolution. Bloemendaal in Holland. A house
    with windows in the kitchen and lavender
    in the yard. By now I know three ways to say apple.

14. There are countries for which we have no passport.
    I sound out words for the little boy who can't see.

15. I am a woman who leaves her husband, finds the way back with
    pockets of sea glass.
    Spirits speak in the house with mango trees and a sky of fire.

16. I live in a pine grove by a field of grass waving in the wind and
    love the land.
    One morning something lifts like smoke and disappears in the sky.
    The red fox crosses into the meadow through a gate of trees.

THE SUGARING CABIN

Coming out of these endless woods in Vermont
as if over a path of ashes I arrive at a clearing
with a small cabin, an open door. Inside
it's swept clean, empty except for sugaring tools
and a long list in an unknown hand penned
on the wooden door, someone else's story
of weather and each year's yield—how many
gallons of syrup a stranger made in this cabin
in the woods:

> ' 76 damn poor year
> ' 77 no weather
> ' 78 waited two weeks for sap . . .

I read the words aloud like a litany
until they grow in me like this practice of doing
year after year, the ways of knowing;
can I be the snow, the emptying trees
tethered to their sapping tubes, giving
and giving? The things a person thinks
about as the sugar comes to boil . . .

These are our gestures:
after the cold nights this waiting
for days to warm, waiting for the rise and fall
to start the sap flow. There's listening for the blue voice,
the gathering, then finally, in its long low pan
the boiling starts. An amber smell soaks the air,
infuses me, like this preparing room, with the possibility

of a place that knows nothing other than sugar
and the boiling that takes its own time,
aromatic back into the darkness.

AT THE HEART OF THINGS
For Thich Nhat Hanh

I go through the simplest tasks
of the day lightened
as the Buddhist spirit of
mindfulness expresses itself
in folding clothes
one warm linen sleeve
lying against another
the cut grass
in full fragrance around me
as I gather peonies
for the table.
Their tall green stems
languish in the water
heads resting heavily
against the bowl's rim
as if under the weight
of a long remembered sorrow.

On the kitchen counter
basil for tonight's pesto,
garlic and walnut's
sharp woody smell
still on the cutting board
the boiling water's steam
condenses on the window glass
and I realize how surely
these are nothing
compared to the abundant task
of gathering all this love.

NIGHT WALK ·

Loosed from the laughter, fire,
familiar dishes by the sink inside
you choose the night walk
where everything is alive with possibility.
On the road the same cold wind
that meets your face
whispers over leaves
like memory reduced to a hand
and how it touched you.
With a whoosh some wild thing
distinguishable only as shadow
jolts across the road;
the sky luminous and alive
rolls from under cloud
while in moonlight deer bathe blue
against the shadow shielded earth
dark and knowing. A hoot, a howl,
in the seductive intimacy of the immaterial
sounds dissolve and reform
every possible someone at the corner
until the bear again becomes a bush
and the road begins to turn toward home.

WHAT THE SILENCE FEEDS

"eats silence like bread."
—Marge Piercy

After the tea pot whistles
and boiling water rushes
from kettle to cup steaming,
as the tea steeps, inside
I find what feeds me
in the gap between sounds.
Mourning doves murmur,
their calls returning to silence
behind a flap of wings.
Snow falls somewhere.

In the cold, breath forms colors,
shapes, and a presence in the stillness
broken only by the whoosh of time passing—
but deeper even the secret frequency
like a distant whir, the universe at work,
and how else to partake of its extravagant
musings except in the long silence?
I eat it like bread into a place where all
is relinquished, where disguises drop away,
where we ourselves are poured
out of the temporal bowl
clear as water.

IF EVER THERE WAS ANYTHING TOO BEAUTIFUL FOR THIS WORLD

If ever there was anything too big
and too beautiful for this world
it's my plumbago, a sprawling treeful
of cornflower blue trumpet
blossoms cascading everywhere.
Loves the light on this terrace
the way it takes right over, and must have
what the bees love—so many,
sweet flowers abuzz

this tree's like a woman
in a polka dot dress,
shimmers in the breeze
like a Marilyn Monroe with
too much color and too much glow,
she's a beacon, arms wide-
open to the sun and moon,
a dazzler all green and blue,
but she's a blaze spreading
everywhere, these branches,
they're exploding like fireworks,
takes your breath away

and she doesn't care,
sheds petals everywhere, makes a mess,
they stick in my hair, grab on my dress till
I'm blooming too, bemused and new

as anyone whose been touched
by who knows what
but everyone's asking
what happened to you?

THE TWITTERING MACHINE

A snake slithers across the path. Was it Paris that spring,
chestnuts in bloom, air of a new season, a room?

Paris was a dream. History, the proverbial story, all things
passing away. The red dress, a bag of apples, hope.
Two rooms and a bath, flowers in the garden. Offerings.
Are they useless? Could we have built the perfect house?

A few pieces of fruit, books on the table, a pen. Mozart
or Brahms. You see how it starts. Something needs
to be protected. Stones gathered for an altar.
Our house is the house of the world.
Birds twitter toward a sweet smell from the brambles.
The mountains blue again, leafless trees rising
like a formation of soldiers coming over the ridge.

The news is all shock and awe till I'm forced to lose myself
in silence, in the elasticity of time. Should the door open
or close? Should I go out or stay in? Should I pray?
Mourn for the messages of ten thousand years in rubble?

We fetch water from the well, drink, bathe, boil. There could be
steps off the path into the other world where the trees are transparent
and glitter with light. Time passes. Wind loose over the pasture
bows the field grass. How shall our praise be sturdy enough
to last? Soft, the evening air is soft. Can you feel it?
Can you see the stars?

VISITING THE FIRST BAPTIST CHURCH AT EASTER TIME

Cast us into the sea of forgiveness, Lord, the preacher says,
the congregation calling yes, amen, raising their hands in the air
as if to feel the presence the preacher says is
right here, right now and the place surely is alive with
something I've never seen in my church where people sit quietly
or are down on their knees for the General Confession. No one
here is quiet as the preacher shouts *make a joyful noise unto the Lord*
and they're calling out right along with him *praise, praise, hallelujah!*

They're riding high on whatever is coming into being, riding on it,
reveling in it, glory it's carrying us right to the brink, to the very banks
of the water so we could almost put our hands in the cool liquid
of absolution, splash it on our faces and he's telling us *take it home brothers*
and sisters, it's the spirit of the Lord and you can take it wherever you go.

And suddenly I see in the heat of arousal, in the midst of this ocean
of *yes Lords* any leader could say *do this in the name of God*
and could name just about anything—go in peace brothers and sisters
or smash the Buddha statues or drive a car bomb into the crowd or
sing and pray with me and we will be delivered and people might ride
on the freight train of zeal still saying *yes Lord* no matter what because
they've felt the real time foot stomping ardor in their bodies not in some
other heavenly promised land but here, tonight, the breath of God hot

with song and just then the preacher cries out *are you experiencing*
the miracle yet? Are you having a break through? It doesn't matter
to where or through what, this is something way beyond location.
He tells us *take it with you. Take it with you whereever you go.*

After the service my friend who has trouble seeing in the dark backs the
car into a ditch. No amount of rocking back and forth is working it out
when some men in a pick-up come by and say no problem we can handle this.
They hook up the bumper and we watch the whole thing hoisted straight up
out of the trench, straight up into the night, free, and light as a feather.

GRATITUDE

The plane glides
across the sky
trailing puffs
of a white message
silver shines and glints on blue
and what if a person
could do what planes do
move above clouds
carry their weight
with grace
fly low
over water
and land without
wobbling in a new place
what if we could
also shed
all that holds us
down
rise and
descend with ease
what if we could sail
or simply walk
on water

THE HAWKS COME BACK

The hawks come back
wide wings over the pines
these seekers and finders
soar and swoop,
where the wind
bears down over the grasses
rippling in the sun.

What shall I do to accustom my eyes
to the new light?
We feel our way up through darkness
for so long, used to the rough ground,
we're hardly strong enough to hold
the pure world.
How is it we're found—
so much in spite of what we choose
or have chosen, our questions
with their flimsy answers—
we're taken and plunged again
and again into radiance
until what once seemed to beckon
only as elusive dazzle
now wants to be the necessary order.
Oh, tell me, how can I
open my arms
wide enough?

SUFI DANCING

We whirl as the dervishes do,
surrendering, circling
moving with the music
faster
and faster
its rhythm in our feet
our outstretched arms
the spinning air,
the driving beat
revolving, whirling
do we feel what the earth feels
surrounded by stars
springs percolating
rivers rushing
deserts dry, hot,
expectant,
the breathing wind,
ecstatic trees
do we feel what the earth feels
its patient elevation
its perpetual willingness
to turn and turn
and go on turning?

ON THE OLD ROAD

Once a thin line of horses came out of the night
and you thought you saw
wings close quietly at their sides
but then they disappeared back into the dark,
to the other side of the road
away from the car's headlights.

You are everywhere looking for a sign,
for the hand of God to lift you up like the sea
lifts the waves, everywhere looking
for something wonderful folded in the darkness
like a code you might cipher,
teasing out words that could teach you
to fix broken things, what makes light.
Just as you flavor tea with sage,
gather wild rosemary sprigs,
season lamb with coarse salt and garlic
you want to know how to be
like the rocks that rise up rounded
by so much water passed over them,
make sense of how we give ourselves to this world.
You're like anybody who asks for clouds,
who likes some white punctuation
to all that sky.

CAVANKERRY'S MISSION

Through publishing and programming, CavanKerry Press connects communities of writers with communities of readers. We publish poetry that reaches from the page to include the reader, by the finest new and established contemporary writers. Our programming brings our books and our poets to people where they live, cultivating new audiences and nourishing established ones.